"It's OK, Joe," said Mum. "Tom lives somewhere on this street. We'll find it."
So they set off.

"No," said Joe.

"No!"
said Joe.

"NO!"
said Joe.

They had come to the end
of the street.

Then they saw it: Tom's house.

Joe didn't notice the door opening slowly . . .

And Joe went in.

And Mum went home.

I hope Joe will be all right . . .
Of course he will – it's only a party!
But what if he's REALLY unhappy?

Two hours later . . .

Knock! Knock! Mum went in . . .

"Hi, Mum, I've had a GREAT time!"

"Oh good," said Mum.

"I was wondering, Joe, if you'd like
to have a party on your birthday?"

"YES, PLEASE!"

said Joe.

Some other books
by Anthony Browne